Three Not-So-Typical Princess Stories

by Carmela LaVigna Coyle
illustrated by Mike Gordon
and Carl Gordon

Princesses Rule! Three Not-So-Typical Princess Stories

www.risingmoonbooks.com

Composed in the United States of America
Printed in China

Edited by Theresa Howell
Designed by David Jenney

FIRST IMPRESSION 2007 Borders Exclusive
ISBN 13: 978-0-87358-945-1
ISBN 10: 0-87358-945-9

Do Princesses Wear Hiking Boots?

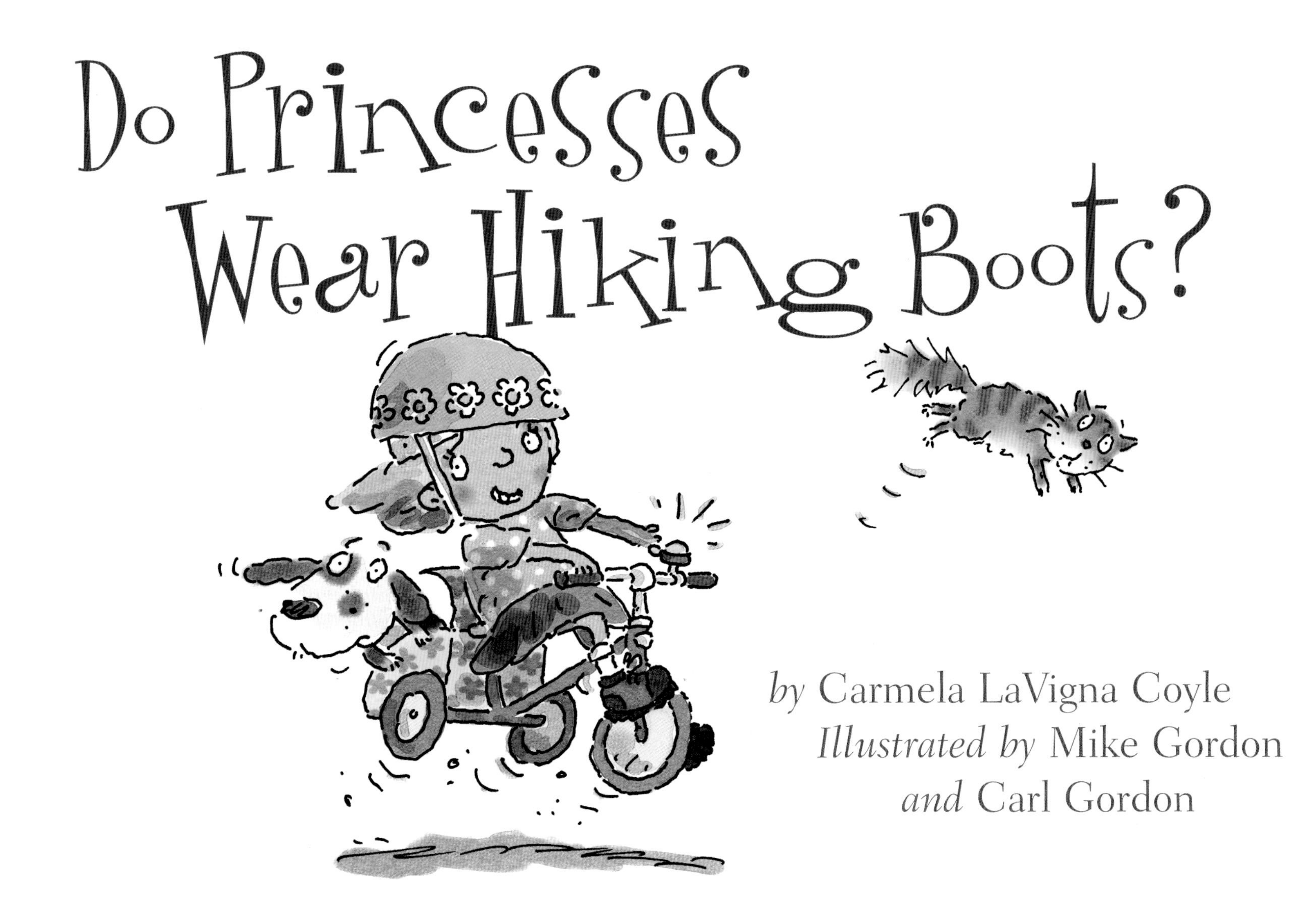

by Carmela LaVigna Coyle
Illustrated by Mike Gordon
and Carl Gordon

Mommy, do princesses wear hiking boots?

When they wish to take the scenic routes.

Do princesses ride tricycles?

Yes, even two-wheel bicycles.

Do princesses climb trees?

Is there a better way to catch the breeze?

Do princesses like to walk in the rain?

That's one of the things they learn at school.

Do princesses eat the crusts of their bread?

They dance through the puddles without refrain!

Do princesses play in the sand and dirt?

If they're wearing jeans and a messy old shirt.

Do princesses have to do any chores?

They clean their drawers and sweep their floors.

Mommy, do princesses have to follow the rules?

They save them for the ducks instead.

Do princesses have a favorite vegetable?

They find them all delectable.

Do princesses drink sparkling punch?

They prefer lemonade with lunch.

When princesses laugh, do they sometimes snort?

They have manners of every sort.

Do princesses cry and make a fuss?

They have bad hair days just like us.

Do princesses snore when they fall asleep?

After they've counted 500 sheep.

Mommy, do princesses seem at all like me?

Look inside yourself and see...

"A princess is
a place in your heart."

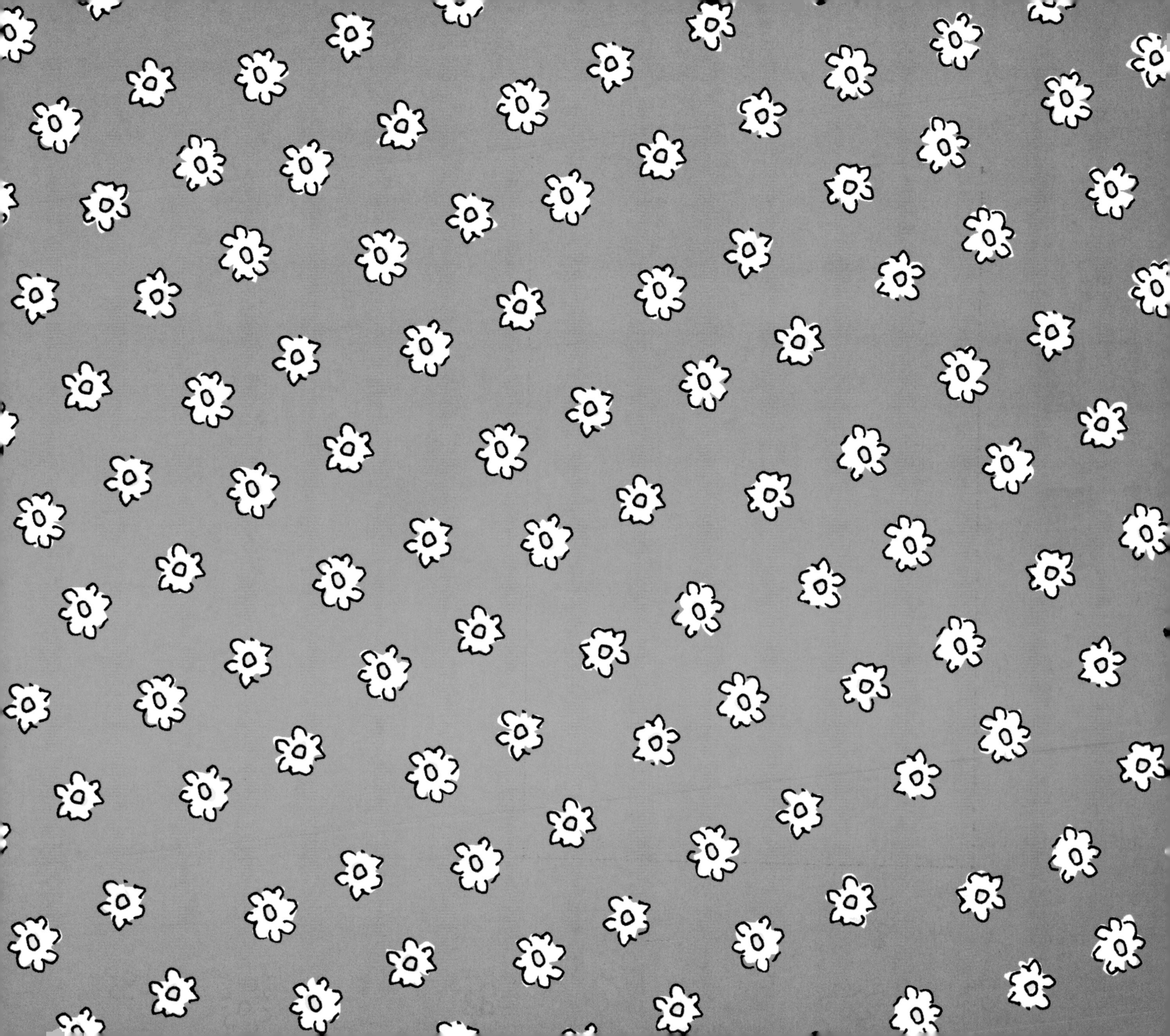

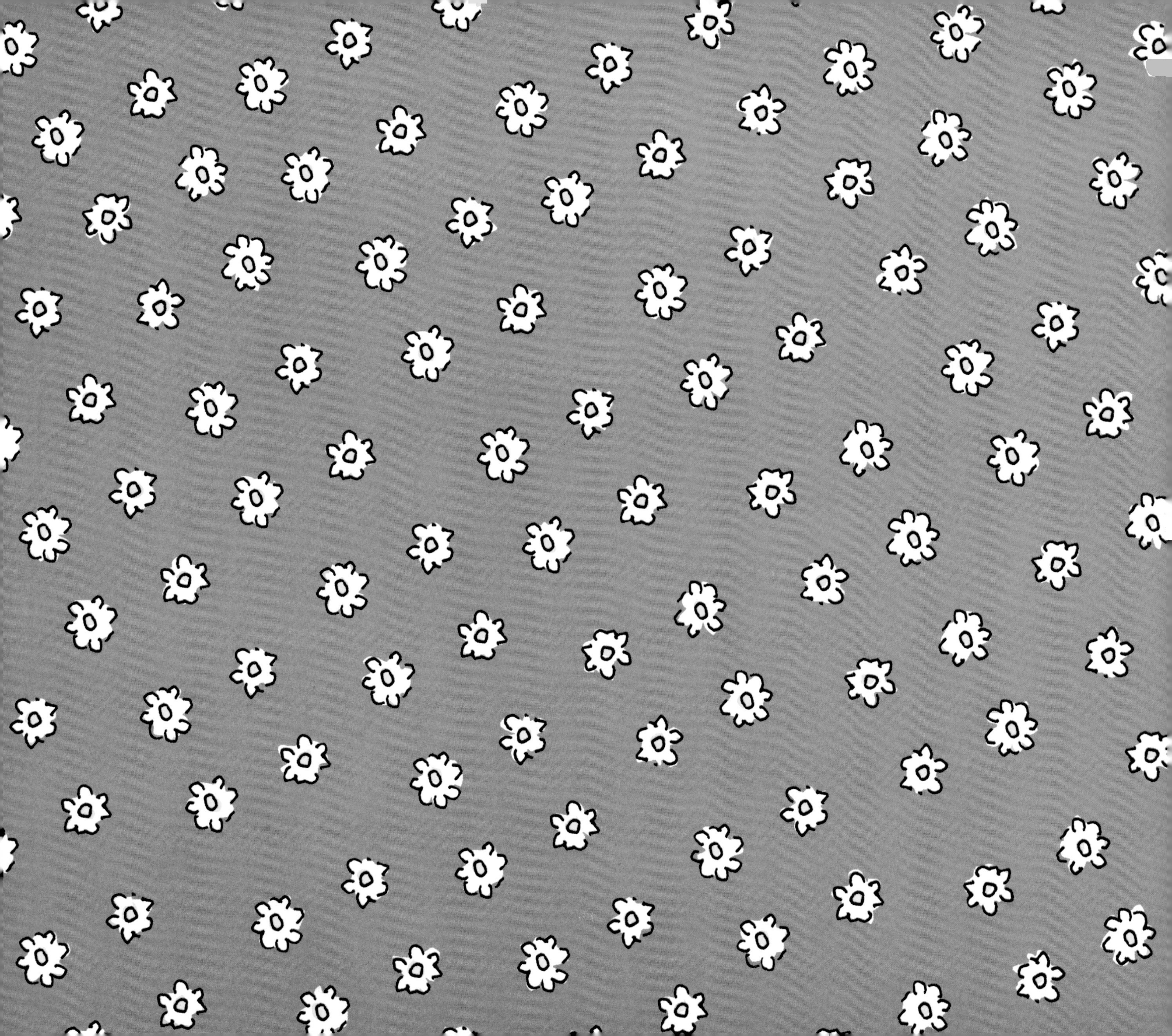

Do Princesses Really Kiss Frogs?

By Carmela LaVigna Coyle

Illustrated by Mike Gordon
and Carl Gordon

rising moon

Daddy, what do princesses wear on a hike?

As long as it's sensible, they wear what they like!

How does she carry her water and snack?

She carries her things in her favorite backpack.

What does she see when she looks in the creek?

Hold my hand, and you take a peek.

Daddy, do princesses really kiss frogs?

They'd much rather kiss
their very own dogs.

Do princesses stop to smell the flowers?

They've been known to do that for hours.

What if a bee lands on the end of her nose?

The bee must have thought that her nose was a rose!

Will she meet a dragon when she comes 'round the bend?

Oh! That would be fun for us all to pretend.

Do princesses keep all the rocks that they find?

Maybe we'll ask if the ranger would mind.

Do princesses like to climb on the boulders?

I think you'd see better from the top of my shoulders.

What if a princess gets hungry and tired?

Then I'd say a treat and a rest are required.

Do princesses dangle their toes in the river?

If they don't mind getting a bit of a shiver!

Will princesses get to see rabbits and deer?

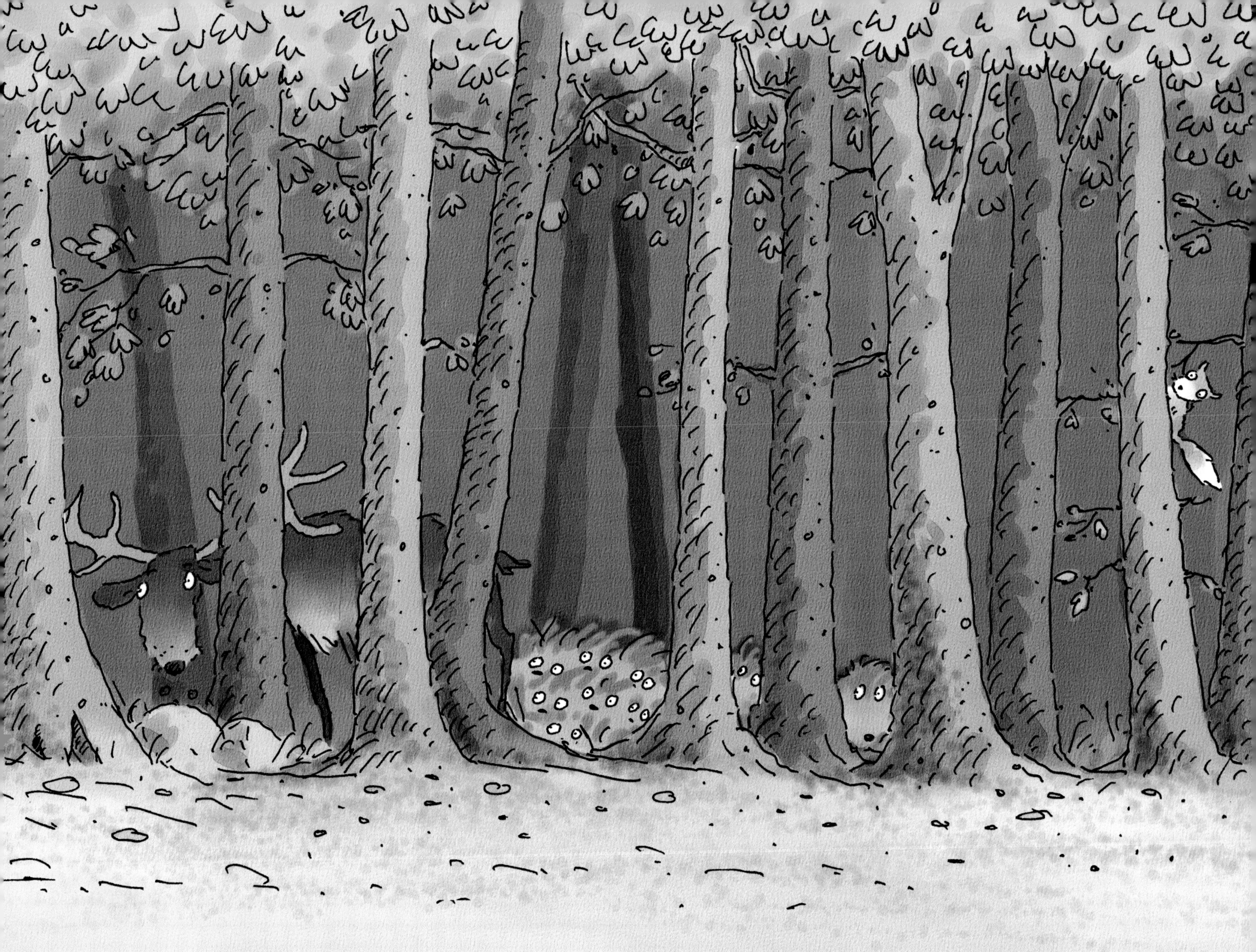

You never know what they might see and hear.

Daddy! Is that a REAL cowboy
hiking this way?

As real as this princess
with me today!

Oh Daddy, look at the view!

There's something about it that reminds me of you!

A princess by nature...

Scavenger Hunt

The princess is going on a scavenger hunt! Can you help her find all the things listed below as she hikes through the book?

You can go on your own scavenger hunt, too. Before going on a walk with your family and friends, make your own checklist of things to look for. You never know what you might see and hear.

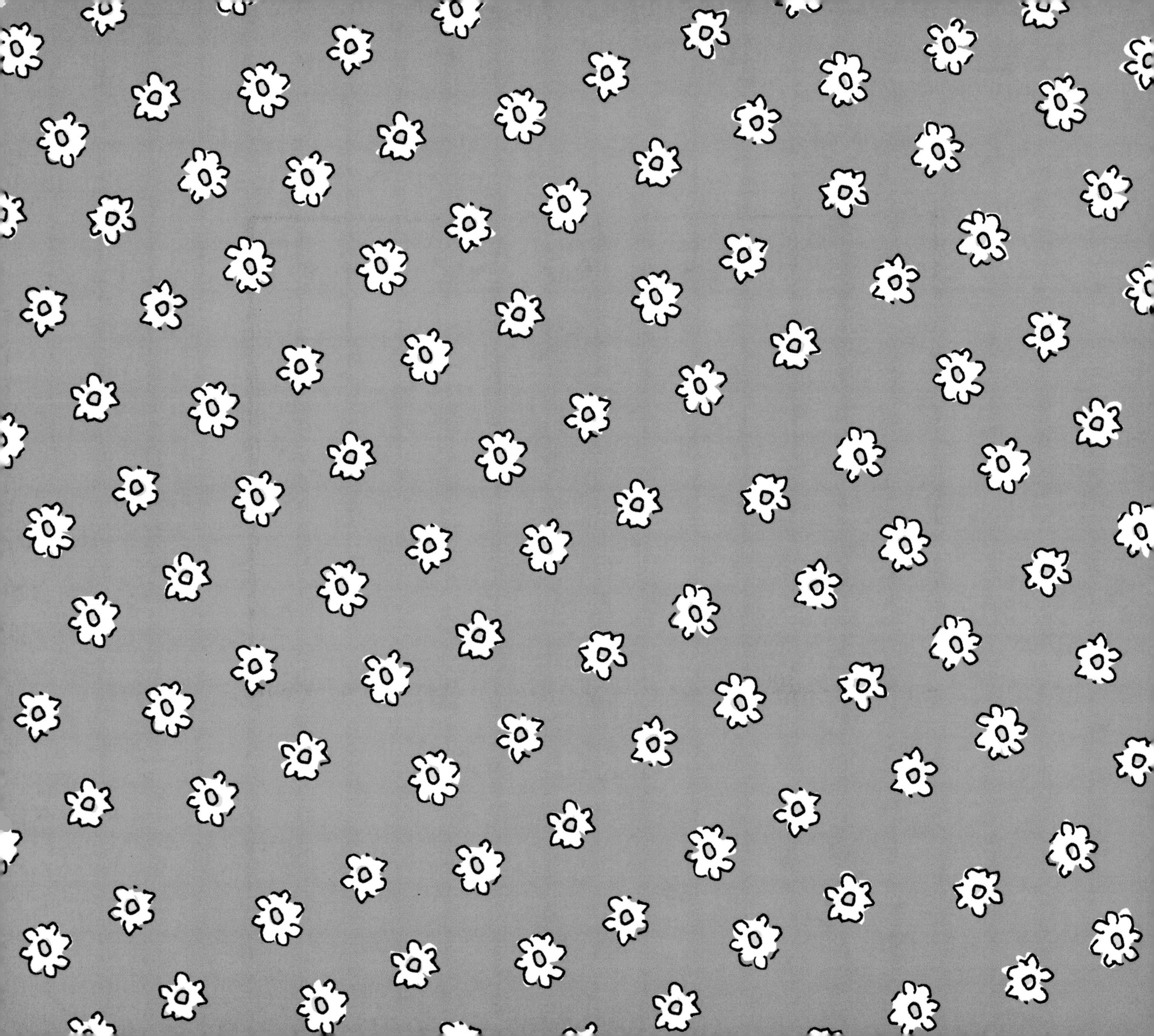

Do Princesses Scrape Their Knees?

Carmela LaVigna Coyle

illustrated by Mike Gordon
and Carl Gordon

Rising Moon

HEY, SIS, can I play with you today?

I guess that would be okay.

What's it called when you fall head-over-heels?

Princesses call them triple cartwheels.

Will Mom let you skate on the living room floor?

Somehow I think I'd be shooed out the door.

Do princesses put Band-Aids®
on their scraped knees?

Princesses can put them wherever they please!

Do you ever get butterflies
inside your belly?

Sometimes my knees feel like they're made out of jelly.

How do you stay in that yoga position?

Ommmm...I keep my muscles in good condition!

Are you going to kick that ball into the goal?

I'm going to try with my whole heart and soul!

Do princesses ever belly flop?

Sometimes they land with a royal ***ker-plop!***

How many times can YOU spin on the ice?

Spinning just ONCE *would be oh-so nice.*

Are you going to walk
on your toes everywhere?

That would be more than my piggies could bear!

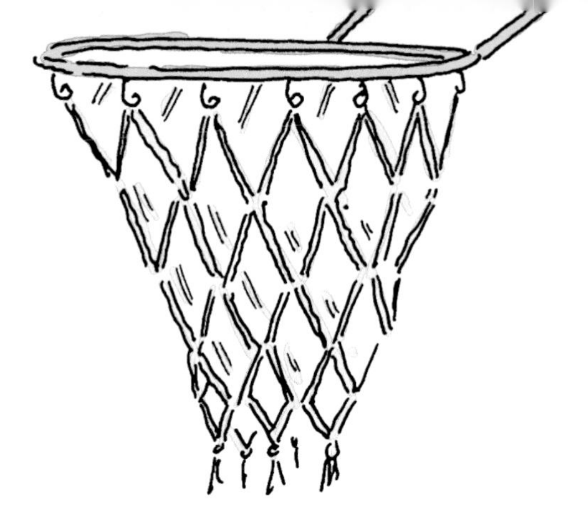

Am I too short to dunk the ball?

With a little help, you're seven feet tall!

Can I ride faster than your speedy pink bike?

It's hard to keep up with my brother's red trike!

Do princesses relax at the end of the day?

That's when they share a chocolate sundae!

When I grow up, can I be sporty like you?

You can do anything you set your mind to.

TOUR DE FRANCE
FINISH